ARCTIC SUMMER

Also by Downs Matthews and Dan Guravich

Polar Bear Cubs
Skimmers

SIMON & SCHUSTER BOOKS FOR YOUNG READERS
Simon & Schuster Building, Rockefeller Center
1230 Avenue of the Americas, New York, New York 10020
Text copyright © 1993 by Downs Matthews
Photographs copyright © 1993 by Dan Guravich
All rights reserved including the right of reproduction
in whole or in part in any form.
SIMON & SCHUSTER BOOKS FOR YOUNG READERS
is a trademark of Simon & Schuster.
Designed by Vicki Kalajian
The text of this book has been set in Versailles 55.
Manufactured in the United States of America

10 9 8 7 6 5 4 3 2 1

Library of Congress Cataloging-in-Publication Data
Matthews, Downs. Arctic summer / by Downs Matthews ;
photographs by Dan Guravich.   p.   cm.
1. Zoology—Arctic regions—Juvenile literature.   I. Guravich, Dan.
II. Title.   QL105.M28   1993   599.0909'13—dc20   92-25376   CIP
ISBN: 0-671-79539-2

ARCTIC SUMMER

BY DOWNS MATTHEWS

PHOTOGRAPHS BY DAN GURAVICH

SIMON & SCHUSTER BOOKS FOR YOUNG READERS

Published by Simon & Schuster

New York   London   Toronto   Sydney   Tokyo   Singapore

Far to the north lies a part of the Earth called the Arctic. Winters there are long and hard.

Years ago, native people in the Arctic thought of winter as a great giant made of frost. When the giant came down from the north, all living things found places to hide. The giant would lie down on the land and it would freeze. He would sleep and the world would become dark and cold. Only the polar bears would walk around.

Then at last a polar bear cub would crawl into the frost giant's nose. The giant would sneeze and wake up. Looking around, he would feel lonesome for his family. He would get up and go back to the north again.

When the frost giant leaves, summer comes. The sun shines day and night. With endless light and warmth, life starts anew. Plants grow leaves. Flowers make seeds. Animals mate and have their little ones.

The plants and animals of the Arctic have no time to waste. Soon snow and darkness will return and life must change or end. Beginning in June and lasting through August, arctic summers are short. Every moment must be lived at top speed.

◁ Arctic cotton grass

△ Rough-legged hawk chicks ▽

Plants make all life possible. In the Arctic, tiny gray mosses and orange lichens creep over rocks facing the sun. Flowering plants make new leaves and send up showy blossoms. They stay close to the ground to hide from the cold wind. The wind blows pollen from one flower to the next. With pollen, a plant can make seed.

In early spring, a geometric moth lays an egg on a purple saxifrage plant. A caterpillar hatches from the egg. It feeds on leaves and flower petals. For thirteen years, the caterpillar freezes each winter and thaws each summer. When it is four-teen years old, it turns into a moth. Next spring, the moth emerges. It lays eggs of its own. The moth visits flowers for nectar to eat. It helps spread pollen from flower to flower so that seeds can form.

In just a few days, the flowers die. Their seeds ripen and fall onto the soil. They lie there all winter until summer comes again. Then they take root and grow into mature plants.

◁ Saxifrage

▽ Arctic lupine and Arctic poppy

Lemmings look like fat furry brown mice. In winter, lemmings stay warm in tunnels they dig under the snow with their strong legs and claws. When summer comes, lemmings pop out of their dens all at once. All of a sudden, lemmings are everywhere. It's as if they had fallen from the sky. Arctic natives call them "sky mice." The lemmings feed on new leaves and roots. They collect and save seeds to eat in the wintertime.

If food is plentiful, lemming males and females mate. In twenty days, a mother lemming gives birth to four to eight young. In twenty-five days, her daughters grow up and mate and have young of their own. Lemming families may have as many as six sets of babies in one summer.

Many arctic animals hunt and eat lemmings. Even so, some lemmings always escape because there are so many of them.

Arctic ground squirrels make large underground dens with lots of tunnels and rooms. For five months in spring and summer, ground squirrels eat constantly. When cold weather comes, they go to sleep for seven months. Native people named the ground squirrel "siksik." That is what its bark sounds like.

The ptarmigan is another plant eater. It is a bird about the size of a small chicken. It eats the buds, berries, and seeds of plants, and insects too.

Because it stays all year in the Arctic, the ptarmigan must keep warm in cold weather. The soft feathery down next to its skin holds in warm air. The tough feathers of its outer coat turn away cold winds. To protect its feet, the ptarmigan wears fluffy snow shoes made of feathers.

As summer begins, the ptarmigan grows a coat of brown feathers to match the rocks and soil. The color of its coat helps the ptarmigan to hide from hungry foxes and snowy owls. Just before winter comes, the ptarmigan gets a white coat to match the snow.

Unlike the ptarmigan, many birds spend only the summer in the Arctic. Pretty little arctic terns fly ten thousand miles from the South Pole to get there. They arrive in May.

Terns are wonderful fliers. A tern can speed through the air or hover in one spot. It uses its flying skill to catch insects on the wing. It dives to the surface of an ocean or lake and catches small fish.

Arctic terns are good parents. They build a nest by scraping a hole in sand or gravel beside a sea or lake. The mother tern lays two or three eggs. Both she and her mate guard the nest bravely. If a person or an animal comes near, terns give loud warning calls. They attack intruders with claws and beaks.

In October, the terns leave the Arctic. They fly back to the Antarctic for another polar summer.

In its thick white coat of fur, the arctic fox is hard to see on the snowy tundra or the frozen sea.

In summer, the arctic fox changes its white coat for one that is brown and gray. No other member of the dog family does this. The fox's coat is so thick and bushy that the animal looks much larger than it really is. An adult fox weighs about the same as a house cat. A newborn fox is no bigger than a kitten.

Red foxes like these puppies are also found in the Arctic. ▷

Arctic foxes live in dens that may have been used over and over for hundreds of years.

For food, foxes depend mostly on lemmings. They sometimes steal birds' eggs and chicks too.

Each spring male and female foxes mate. If food is short, the female may have only five or six pups. If there is lots of food, she may have twelve or more. Yet life is so hard in the Arctic that only a few survive.

The ermine is a small member of the weasel family. An adult male is about twelve inches long, including its tail. Females are even smaller. They are slender enough to enter lemmings' tunnels in pursuit of food.

White in winter, brown in summer, ermines are tireless hunters. No animal is faster or quicker, none braver or tougher. Ermines are always hungry.

When an ermine kills a lemming, it takes the food home to its den in the frozen ground. It puts the meat in its underground icebox and has several meals from it.

Little ermines are born in summer. A year later, they are ready to have babies of their own.

Muskoxen are the wild cattle of the Arctic. Like cows, they eat plants.

In summer, herds of muskoxen graze among the willows and grasses that grow beside creeks and in moist meadows.

To keep warm during winter, muskoxen grow an undercoat of fine brown fleece. On top, they have an overcoat of long straight hair that hangs down to the ground. In summer, they get hot and shed their underwear.

When attacked by wolves, muskoxen form a circle. Young calves stay in the middle where they are safe. The adults face outward. They defend themselves with their sharp horns.

Caribou are members of the deer family. They move back and forth across the Arctic in great herds. Caribou eat mosses and lichens and green plants.

Most caribou spend their winters in forests to the south where trees give protection from the wind and snow.

In spring, for safety from insects and wolves, the females leave the forests. They go down to the seashore where the wind helps keep mosquitoes away. Their calves are born there.

Within an hour after they are born, baby caribou can stand up and walk. Within a day they can run. This helps calves escape from wolves, bears, and eagles.

△ Caribou are as at home in water as on land

For most animals, summer is a time when food is plentiful. But not for polar bears.

Throughout the winter, the huge white polar bears hunt seals on the sea ice. When the ice melts in summer, seals can easily swim away from polar bears. Bears often go hungry.

Before summer begins, polar bears catch many seals. They eat as much food as they can and get fat. Then, when seals are hard to catch, they live off the fat in their bodies.

Polar bears get so hot during the arctic summer that they go swimming to keep cool.

Harp seal females give birth to their pups in early spring. Harp seal mothers swim far south through the open ocean. They go to the ice of a frozen bay. The mothers make holes in the ice. Then they crawl out and give birth to their pups where they are safe from hungry polar bears.

For a few days, baby harp seals wear fluffy white coats of fur. But they grow very fast. Within two weeks, they begin to get dark gray coats. Then they go into the water and teach themselves to swim and catch fish.

As the ice melts, harp seals swim north. They follow schools of fish. They are fast swimmers and can easily catch many fish to eat.

When the sea ice begins to melt, female walruses swim north. They find a place where the ice never melts. There they give birth to their pups. Mothers and pups rest and sleep on blocks of floating ice.

Walrus mothers feed their babies on very rich milk. The pups grow quickly. They soon learn to swim. Then they can dive to the ocean floor with their mothers and learn to eat clams. Walruses suck clams into their mouths the way a vacuum cleaner sucks up dirt from a rug.

Male walruses swim south in summer. They like to lie on a warm beach and sleep. Every few days, male walruses go out to feed on clams and other sea creatures that live on the ocean floor.

As summer ends, male and female walruses get together again to start another family.

For most of the year beluga whales live in the cold arctic seas. *Beluga* is a Russian word meaning "white."

When summer comes, belugas swim into the mouths of rivers that flow into the northern seas. They spend all summer resting and feeding in the warm waters. A beluga uses the food it eats in summer to grow. In winter, it uses the food to keep warm.

Beluga calves are born in early spring. They drink their mothers' rich milk and grow quickly. Soon they are able to catch fish for themselves.

Young beluga whales are gray. When they grow up, they become white. Their white color helps them hide from the killer whales that sometimes hunt them.

When winter comes and the sea begins to freeze, the belugas leave the river mouths. They return to the ice-filled ocean.

At the end of summer, the frost giant comes back to the Arctic. The sky grows dark. Snow falls and ice forms on the lakes and seas. The bitter wind slices across the frozen ground.

The summer animals leave. Arctic terns go south. So do the seals, walruses, and whales. The caribou return to their sheltering trees.

The animals that stay behind find ways to keep warm. Ptarmigan make beds in snow drifts. Foxes hide in their dens. Lemmings build tunnels in the snow.

Now all the animals wait. One day the polar bear cub will find the frost giant's nose and wake him up again. Summer will return to the Arctic. Then, for a little while, the Arctic will once again leap with joyous life.